A RUN IN THE PARK

Travelling in a Strange Land
Gods and Angels
The Rye Man
Stone Kingdoms
The Poets' Wives
The Light of Amsterdam
Oranges From Spain
Swallowing the Sun
The Big Snow
The Healing
The Truth Commissioner

A RUN IN THE PARK

PARK

David Park

BLOOMSBURY PUBLISHING
LONDON · OXFORD · NEW YORK · NEW DELHI · SYDNEY

BLOOMSBURY PUBLISHING
Bloomsbury Publishing Plc
50 Bedford Square, London, WC1B 3DP, UK

BLOOMSBURY, BLOOMSBURY PUBLISHING and the Diana logo
are trademarks of Bloomsbury Publishing Plc

First published in Great Britain 2019

A Run in the Park is an original Radio 4 commission

A catalogue record for this book is available from the British Library

ISBN: HB: 978-1-5266-1997-6; EPUB: 978-1-5266-1998-3

2 4 6 8 10 9 7 5 3 1

Typeset by Integra Software Services Pvt. Ltd.
Printed and bound in Great Britain by CPI Group (UK) Ltd,
Croydon CR0 4YY

To find out more about our authors and books visit www.bloomsbury.com
and sign up for our newsletters

For all those trying to set their souls in motion

Contents

Maurice

I'm a big Bruce Springsteen fan – have seen him live twice – but, no matter how I look at it, there isn't any way I was born to run. And it's not just because my body has gradually morphed into something I struggle to recognise as belonging to me, or one that even remotely conforms to the comforting self-image we all secretly harbour. It's also because I haven't tried running since I was a boy and, if you want the truth, it's something I vaguely associate with the criminal – taking to my heels after scrumping apples, knocking doors and scarpering. And I got through school games lessons on a sick note – generally one I had forged myself.

So this unexpected impulse to take up running and try this Couch to 5K thing goes against the grain of who I am. And when I see runners as I'm driving, I always think they look a bit desperate, like they're running from whatever makes them unhappy. But maybe that's why I'm going to start, because I need to keep one step ahead of my own unhappiness before it catches up with me and I can't shrug it off.

Mina was a Springsteen fan too, but her favourite song was 'Dancing in the Dark'. And of course she had this fantasy that she'd be the one he'd call out of the audience to dance with him on stage. That was just one part of the future she never had. The future we never had. A chance meeting one night with a drunk driver, on her way home from the college where she taught, took all of that away. And what I do feel is cheated. Cheated because we were both a year off our retirements, and with so many plans made about where we were going to travel, the new activities we were going to take up. And it's not like you're playing some game or sport and you can appeal to the referee or umpire and get everything put right. Summon up VAR. So there is no resolution possible, and I don't for a second think that taking up running is going to dull the pain that's locked inside me, but just maybe it will kick-start me into some forward motion. That's all I want right now – just some sense of being able to make it through each coming day.

I read somewhere that loneliness makes you feel cold. Well, I guess that grief is supposed to make you thinner, but I think it's had the opposite effect on me. I was never a Slim Jim, but now too much sitting about, too much weight of introspection and too many ready-made meals have all combined to pile on the pounds. And a Pavlov's dogs thing has started because now I associate food with the ping of the microwave. I was never exactly an unreconstructed man and did my share of household stuff, but Mina did most of the cooking, saw the kitchen as her domain. Even though she's been gone three years, when I'm pottering about in it, it's hard not to be mindful of her absence and that's another reason why I've resorted on too many occasions to fast food. Mostly I use the drive-through, eat in the furthest corner of the car park with music for company.

Fast food. That's a misnomer if there ever was one. Clogging your arteries with gunge as its pleasure shot pumps you with too much fat, calories and cholesterol. Slowing you down. Slowing you down until you feel you're permanently moving in slow motion, and I can feel it inside my head too and I know I'll slip into depression if I don't do something, try to release some of those endorphins

I've been reading about, even though whenever I read or hear the word 'endorphin', I always think of plastic dolphins for some reason. But I've got to keep one step ahead of it or I'll go under. And I can't do that because we have a daughter Rachel and a granddaughter called Ellie and I want to be around for them. If even right now they don't want to be around me.

Until I retired I was an auditor. And, yes, sitting too long staring at a computer has been part of my problem. But it does mean that I'm good at adding things up, at seeing whether the columns tally. So life for me is about understanding gain and loss, about surplus and deficit. About balancing the books. And I've a keen eye for fraud, for knowing when someone or something is being sold short. That was always the problem with Rachel and her choice of partner, and just because love enters the equation doesn't mean that all other considerations get thrown out of the window and you write a blank cheque to the person you've chosen to share your life with.

Neither of us liked Mark, even though Mina was more diplomatic about it and better at hiding her feelings than I ever was. But the more I expressed reservations about the way he treated her, the more

Rachel made excuses for him, always ending her defence with the assertion that we didn't understand him. And in that at least she was right, because I don't understand any man who thinks that love is expressed by selfishness, by drinking too much and, although I never knew for sure, by frightening the person you have chosen to live with. Nor has he ever had a steady job, and some months we bailed them out with money that we didn't ever look to be returned.

Rachel was never the best judge of people. Even in school she would walk away from decent kids and work to get herself accepted into some social circle from which she would subsequently get dumped. I'm no psychologist, but maybe she's someone who needs acceptance from whoever she thinks is least likely to give it. But she's twenty-seven now and so perhaps it's time she grew out of that need, found a better understanding of who's good for her and who's not. And maybe I'm flattering myself, but I like to think I was a good father to her and would be still if she'd let me. But I haven't seen her much since her mother's death – I'm not allowed to just call at their house because she says it's best if she comes round to me. When she does she brings Ellie, who is four now, and while that gives me a great deal of pleasure, I try not to believe that their irregular visits coincide with the times she needs money.

If anything, I'm more convinced than ever that Mark is a lowlife because Rachel seems different – tentative, always metaphorically and literally looking over her shoulder, never really relaxed with Ellie. Telling the child to be quiet and sit beside her when all she wants to do is explore the house. But I can't risk saying anything, because I know the consequences will be even greater distance and a reduction in the already meagre rations I'm allocated. And there's something else I never say to Rachel. Have never told her and didn't tell Mina because she'd have been angry with me. Mark and I have had words. Just after Ellie was born I went round when she was struggling a bit and he was sleeping off a bender. So I woke him and asked if he was taking good care of his wife and child and he gave me a mouthful, and I've never been as close to hitting anyone in my whole life. Most acutely at the moment when he called me Fat Man.

And maybe, despite everything I've said about taking up running, it really all comes down to this. A piece of lowlife called me Fat Man. Because that's when I decided I wasn't going to be that overweight couch potato any more, and it wasn't just about personal vanity or self-preservation but because I understood that I needed to be in good shape as, sooner or later, my daughter and my granddaughter would need me to come running. And I want to be ready, don't want to let them down, because in that moment when I looked at the fixed hatred on his face, I saw someone who wasn't able to control or suppress the anger inside him. And that's something that scares me.

So I'm set to start running. My royal-blue Fusion Pro quick-dry long-sleeve half-zip running tops (extra large) have arrived with two pairs of tracksuit bottoms (also extra large) and a pair of running shoes (size 12). I've tried them on in front of a bedroom mirror and told myself that I don't look ridiculous. But am not entirely sure and then doubt floods in until I stand close to the mirror, let my fingers press against the coldness of the glass, and I tell myself that I'm doing it for Rachel and Ellie, doing it for Mina. Doing it for myself because I have to keep moving forward and ward off this creeping paralysis.

And before long I'm being congratulated by Pauline for having the courage to give it a go, and I like her already because she says all the right things, tells us that we're all going to help each other, that we can do it, even those of us who think we can't, and the programme works if we commit to it — three sessions a week with one rest day in between. For nine weeks. Nine weeks very gradually working up to the final graduation run. And she's telling us of the benefits, and I want to believe her, and when I look around there's all ages and all shapes so I only feel mildly self-conscious. She makes us laugh with a joke about fast-food takeaways and for a second I think she's been spying on me, but then I convince myself that if I'd had a PE teacher like her I might not have forged so many sick notes. Some people have come with a friend or partner, but there are plenty on their own, and as we set off for our first session round the council's playing fields, we are bunched up in a tight group that creates a sense of joint enterprise. A brisk five minutes' walk and then Pauline blows her whistle and we begin our first minute of running. The first spaces open. But what is a minute of running? A scamper out of the rain, a rush for a bus, a scurry towards a slowly closing door. It's only a minute but already there's something not quite right. I'm moving forward but it's more of a shuffle than a stride. And I'm conscious that I'm carrying too much in front of me. I look down and my royal-blue Fusion Pro quick-dry long-sleeve half-zip top makes me look as if I'm carrying a Lambeg drum. I'm still pondering this when the whistle blows and Pauline is walking beside me and asking if I'm OK. I tell her yes and try to say the words without them sounding like air coming out of a balloon.

One minute of running followed by one and a half minutes of walking for a total of twenty minutes. I wonder when she blows her whistle to start running if I can disguise walking so it looks like running. There's something of a slight sideways movement working itself into my motion and I can't help thinking of a ship in a storm where cargo has broken free and is sliding about the hold. Then I'm conscious of someone beside me.

'How's it going?' she asks.

'Not so bad,' I tell her.

Pauline has encouraged us to talk to each other – she says it helps keep our breathing right. But right now I'm not the one able to lead the conversation because the whistle has gone and we're setting off on our final run.

'I'm Catherine – Cathy really.'

I tell her my name is Maurice and try to stop my voice sounding like a heavy breather on the end of a phone.

'Hi Maurice,' she says. 'Longest journeys, single step and all that.'

'Yes,' I say, but all I'm listening for is that final whistle and when it goes I try to hold myself straight as we do our warm-down brisk walk and not yield to the temptation to put my hands on my hips as if I've just run a marathon.

Pauline tells us we've done well, taken that big first step, and she'll see us next session and how important it is to always do one on our own. Then I'm in the car and, even though I'm going back to an empty house, I try to shrug off that loneliness with the comfort that Mina would be pleased I've started to move forward again. And despite everything that's happened, I'm off the couch, up and running.

Cathy

I think Maurice needs a little encouragement – that's why I've been talking to him, and I'm happy to run at his pace even though I think I might be able to go a little faster. But tortoise and hare and all that. And there's something vaguely nostalgic about having a man's heavy breathing in my ear – something I haven't heard in over ten years since my conscious uncoupling with my husband, although there wasn't anything particularly conscious about it on my part, because with no prior warning he went off with his work colleague. And if you want the truth, there hadn't even been much heavy breathing in the years before he left.

Maurice still has the price tags on the soles of his running shoes and sometimes his breathing is less amatory in my imagination and more like a boiling kettle that hasn't enough water in it. But he seems a decent soul and he'll have to forgive me for remembering what a woman once said about her encounter with someone of similar build that it was like having a wardrobe fall on top of her and being poked by the key. But then again I never think about wardrobes without remembering that sometimes they lead you into surprisingly beautiful and mysterious snow-covered worlds.

It's the story I like reading to the children in the library book club most of all. So many of the new children's books, worthy as they are, are driven by the most fashionable social issues and I think children sometimes just need stories. Need lions and evil witches. Need mystery and wonder. In fact we all need stories, and although it probably labels me as some stereotype of an old-school, old-fashioned, liver-spotted, musty librarian, I've never found anyone better at telling a story than Charles Dickens. I know my colleagues think it's hilariously weird, but when I go to London I always visit his house in Doughty Street. They have his desk and chair where he wrote and even part of the prison grille of the Marshalsea debtors' prison where Dickens's father was locked up.

And there's something else to do with Dickens in my head right now. It's a line from *A Tale of Two Cities* that's running round my head, and it's 'recalled to life', which Dickens uses to refer to Dr Manette's release from the Bastille and of course Sydney Carton's regeneration through love. Recalled to life – that's what I feel and why I'm here running. I had a scare, a small lump in my breast, a referral and then a long anxious wait where you torment yourself before the scans and tests. Everything finally got declared OK, but an experience like that frightens you at first and when it's over you want to do whatever it takes to give yourself the best chance of staying well. And you want to embrace life more fully. Want, regardless of how much time has passed or whatever the hurt and disappointment of previous experience, to love and be loved. Because no matter how long you spend on your own, it's not easy to get used to the singleness of it, just like the Joni Mitchell song about the bed being too big, the frying pan too wide. But most of all because there's no one to hold you when you're frightened. No one to tell you it will be all right.

I never told anyone about the scare, not even our daughter Zara who lives with her husband and their child in Australia. Skype never seems the best means of saying things that are important. So everything on it is mostly jolly and upbeat, my four-year-old grandson Patrick used by Zara to fill the awkward gaps until he gets bored talking to a woman he's never met and wanders off. Sometimes it feels like watching a foreign film with no subtitles, because you're trying to read things from the faces, ponder the silent gaps when we both run out of small talk. And despite the happy images and my daughter's face in front of me, there's no way of hiding the realisation that she's on the other side of the world and that our lives are largely strangers to each other. What's the point then of sending an announcement like the health scare I had spinning through the ether when you don't know how it will be received or impact on her far-off life.

There are times when I think that, although she's never said it outright, Zara somehow blames me for separating from her father, even though he was the one who went off with someone else. She was always a bit of a daddy's girl and sometimes I've sensed that she thinks it was something I did or didn't do that caused the split. And although she tried to keep it from me, I know he's been out there to see her with his new partner, and that hurt. Hurt a lot and in a childish way made me want to magic a new partner for myself. Good for the goose, good for the gander and all that.

I'm thinking of trying online dating but I've heard some scare stories and another scare is exactly what I don't need right now. So I'm nervous about it. Sometimes if you want things too much or try too hard, life takes pleasure in denying you, so for these nine weeks I'm going to concentrate only on running and staying well. We've started gently and in this second week we're doing ninety seconds of running and two minutes of walking. This easy pace means we're mostly pretty bunched up and, abandoning Maurice briefly, I've already spoken to quite a few of the group – to Ciara who wants to be a firefighter and is in training to pass the fitness test; to Brian the accountant and Elise the classroom assistant; to Brendan and Angela who tell me they want to look good in their wedding photographs; and to Maureen who's bored with watching TV every night. But I've never spoken to the young woman wearing a hijab because she seems keen to run on her own and I don't want to intrude.

And the library keeps me busy too, despite the cutbacks and the struggle for funding. It's true no one ever takes out Dickens or the classics any more. Sadly it's all mostly according to stereotype – romantic fiction for the women, crime fiction for the men, with a gender crossover for biographies and books that show you how to do something. And of course the computers. They're in constant use. Kids doing homework, people who have no home connection accessing the internet, and more and more people seeking help with filling in their PIP forms or doing something else demanded by officialdom. So it's not just about tidying books on shelves or stamping books – not that we actually stamp anything any more – but it sometimes feels like we're social workers as well. Even though it's not in our job descriptions, helping with appeals, advising people how to access things they need to live in the modern world. And sometimes too it feels as if we're increasingly living in a tale of two very different cities, two different experiences of life, where some are always just getting by.

So if I had to pick a book for these days we live in it would be *Hard Times*, and that's maybe because I volunteer at the weekend helping with a food bank, set up in our church hall. Every time I hear about people having their claims turned down and others stumbling as a last resort into payday loans, it makes me think of that prison grille in Doughty Street, think of the prison in which debt and desperation confine you.

And if anyone was able to look inside my head, they might see that in its most secret parts I sometimes think of myself as a kind of Sissy Jupe, throwing off the Gradgrinds of this world, happy to dwell in the world of the imagination but able too to lend my hand to what is practical and right. Maybe that's one of the reasons I'm reluctant to go online, be judged by how I look when I know that the totality of who I am consists of so much more.

Maurice tells me he has a daughter, and after telling him about mine in Australia, I asked him where she lived, and it seems she's only a few streets away. 'But she might as well be in Australia,' he said so quietly I almost didn't hear him. He didn't elaborate and I didn't ask. I think his breathing's getting better and there's less sideways movement in his running, but he's never going to find it easy. But fair play to him and fair play to all of us for giving it a go, and Pauline's really encouraging, always telling us we're doing great and taking turns to run with each of us. She's very insistent that we must do our third independent run of the week.

Running on your own is probably the hardest part of the programme – when it's something you've never done before, it's easy to feel a little self-conscious, particularly in leggings that make you think you're out in public in your knickers — so, taking up Pauline's suggestion, a small group of us who live quite close have decided to join up. There's me, Maurice, Brian, Maureen and a Polish woman called Zofia who has her own cleaning business. Following Pauline's advice, we've all invested in high-viz tops so we're a luminous little phalanx running the city's streets. And we're only one of many, and sometimes when we encounter what I think of as proper runners, they acknowledge us as if we too have been granted admittance to their exclusive club. On these runs we replace Pauline with Laura on an app, who starts by congratulating us on having the willpower to reach Week Two and having overcome the first hurdle and then proceeds to tell us when to run and when to walk.

I might be wrong but I'm pretty sure our run eventually takes us past Maurice's daughter's house because he turns his head towards it and scrutinises it intently as he shuffles by. It's not an attractive house and there is an air of neglect, from the untidy pocket of front garden to the dingy-looking net curtains screening the windows. I've no time to ponder these things because Laura is telling us we have only one ninety-second run left, exhorting us to keep a nice steady pace and assuring us that we can do it. When we finish she congratulates us again and tells us it wasn't easy. I am already fond of Laura, even though I only ever get to hear her voice, but she's encouraging, personal, and she sounds like someone who doesn't judge you, only wants what's best for you.

My daughter Zara has told me that she's pregnant in our latest Skype and I can see in her face that she's frightened because she had such a hard time giving birth to Patrick and because she lost her first in early pregnancy. See it in her face, but I can't talk about it or reach out my arms to her, so instead we do that jolly congratulations thing, try to fill the spaces, hush our fears with meaningless small talk. There is a television or radio playing somewhere in the background and while we chat Zara sometimes turns her gaze away from the camera to briefly look elsewhere. I say her hair is nice and she tells me that she hasn't done anything to it, then describes how well Patrick is getting on in nursery school.

And I want to cry but can't until her face finally disappears into the darkness. Because I know that I too am a disembodied voice offering encouragement, reassuring someone far away that she's doing well, that she can do it, and I want to tell her that

I too know what it is to be frightened, so I can share her fears. Then, when her face finally fades from the screen, I am filled with a sense of unspeakable distance, reminded of all the burgeoning absences in my life. In the sudden silence I talk to my only child, tell her everything that I couldn't say.

Brendan and Angela

Brendan

It was Angela's idea that we signed up to the Couch to 5K. She says we want to look our very best on our wedding day – a day she's been planning for a year like a military campaign. Part of me has started to think I'm actually in a kind of war – a war against wedding planners, a war with family over who should or should not be invited, a war with venues, photographers and bridesmaids. I'm just about ready to wave a white flag, except there's no provision for that in Angela's spreadsheets and battle plans. She's resolutely 'Onwards to victory' and doesn't always believe in taking prisoners. But I'm enjoying the running, so it's turned out to be one of her better ideas. In this third week we're edging up to three minutes of running followed by three minutes of walking. And I feel good after the sessions, self-righteously good but also physically good. Pauline always keeps it light and makes sure we have a bit of a laugh, but I'm glad I packed in smoking some years ago because my lungs need all the free flow of air that I can muster. I've discovered too that I like the rhythm of running, and because I interact with people all day in my job as a nurse, it gives me private time, time to think. And even though Pauline encourages us to talk, I like to stride out a little and just occupy my own space.

Angela

Yes, I do want the day to be perfect and, despite what Brendan thinks, that won't just happen, so I'm leaving nothing to chance. Right down to this running. This running that I hate because I don't like anything that hurts and all that 'no pain, no gain' sounds like the stupidest type of thinking. And although he doesn't know it, we're also going to take some dance lessons so that when we have our first married dance, we don't look like the *Strictly* equivalent of two left feet. Despite Brendan's occasional lack of enthusiasm, there's nothing wrong with wanting things to be perfect, aiming to start off the rest of your life together in the best way possible. And I know he does too underneath it all, because I could never be with anyone willing to accept second best. But this week we've had words because he's started to run ahead and I think we should stay together, like a team, like a partnership. And sometimes he's run with Ciara, the young woman who wants to be a firefighter, and for all I know maybe he's fantasising about her rescuing him from a burning building, slinging him over her shoulders and making their way down the ladder to some permanent shared safety.

Brendan

Angela runs a little bit slowly for me and I want to encourage her, but it's not as if we're on a tandem or that we have to go through life joined at the hip. And I want to get better at running, to push myself a little. Otherwise what's the point? Angela doesn't like running because she's never really had to do anything that gives her grief, and because she's from a wealthy family who make so much money from property in this city, from wheeling and dealing, that they've always had someone else do the things they don't want to dirty their hands with. So they pay to have their wealth protected by accountants and lawyers, their house secured by experts, their garden tended – even the dogs get walked by someone else – and if the word on the street is correct – and the street is where I'm from – they haven't always been averse to employing muscle when encountering some recalcitrant problem.

Angela and me are a bit of an *Across the Barricades* love story, except in this case what separates us isn't the old cliché of religion, because let's face it, only the cave-dwellers in this city bother very much about that any more. No, the gulf that separates us is money – I didn't say class because in my eyes my family from a terrace house has as much, if not more, class than hers, despite the money that drips from them. And I know that her father Aidan has constantly thrown cold water on our relationship, sown every possible seed of doubt and hoped his daughter's infatuation with someone from the wrong side of the tracks and who works as a nurse for the National Health Service would eventually fizzle out. It must have really broken his heart when Angela told him we're getting married. And fair play to her: for all her cosseted upbringing she doesn't bend easily, and doesn't ever get bullied, not even by her father. So she's been loyal to me and that's something I value and I think we can make a go of this if we're allowed to.

Just like we can make a go of this running if we stick at it. And it's a chance to try and clear my head from some of the sadness I see in my job, try to think about the future I'm running towards. And the truth is I've been having doubts recently. Doubts about the type of life I'm planning to sign up to. And I don't like the way my family felt uncomfortable when they went to a get-to-know-you meet-up with hers after we announced our engagement, right from the moment when they received a printed invitation in the post. Like they were being summoned to the big house, to bloody Buckingham Palace. So much so that my mother insisted they arrive in a taxi rather than their twelve-year-old rust bucket of a car. Angela and her mother – and her mother is someone I've always liked – did their best to welcome them and make them feel at home. But hard to feel at home amidst the champagne and where their own house could probably have fitted inside the kitchen. And my father means no harm but he keeps saying I've done well for myself, as if I've been given a meal ticket for life.

But money's nothing to do with why I love Angela. Love isn't something you can ever begin to explain, so forgive me if I don't try. Just let me just say I love it when she smiles with her eyes, the way she's kind to my mother and how when she grills up cheese on toast she thinks she's demonstrated the epitome of culinary skill. I met her, slightly ironically, after the Gay Pride march in the city centre – my sister Catriona is gay and I'd gone on the march to support her. Afterwards in a bar Angela assumed I was too, until during a convoluted, cross-purposes conversation she discovered I wasn't. That was the start and somehow two years later we're going to get married.

When I'm running, a space seems to clear in my head and I'm able to think. Ciara doesn't want to talk either so we just stride out in contented silence. But into that silence flow some of the doubts that I spoke of. And they begin with the wedding itself and a growing realisation that Aidan intends to use it to show off his status to the world, to throw so much money at it that it becomes a glossy-magazine supplement in itself. He's talking of arriving with Angela in a helicopter, about hiring some big-name chart-topping musician, massive firework displays and for all I know, gold-painted doves flying out of the priest's cassock. And none of this is what I want, and sooner rather than later I'm going to have to tell Angela, try to put the brakes on before this juggernaut hurtles unstoppably over the edge into disaster for both of us.

But maybe the wedding's only the tip of the iceberg because my doubts are about more than this. And if we let him control the first day of our future life together, shape it in the way he wants with money, then what's to stop him trying to shape everything that comes after? How can we ever be independent of his vision for us, but will Angela ever be willing to live our life together without all the stuff to which she's become accustomed?

Angela

I'm not going to admit it to Brendan, because it was my idea in the first place, but I don't like running. I like to think I've kept myself in decent shape and use the gym at home, but there is something different about this. It's a bit – I'm not sure what the word is – maybe 'raw' comes close, and it's a complete mystery to me how anyone runs a marathon. And I'm competitive, need to be good at the things I do, so it's a bit of an unwelcome surprise and a disappointment that so far I've found it difficult and we're only on Week Three. I thought it would come naturally, that everything would just flow – I mean, how hard can it be to run? – but I know now that if I'm going to complete the programme, I'm going to have to make a real effort. And I don't want Brendan ever to think I'm a spoilt little rich girl, so there's no way I'm giving up on this. God bless her, but Pauline's a bit too jolly-hockey-sticks for my liking, and when I ask Brendan what he talks to Ciara about, he says 'nothing', that they don't talk, but when I see them up ahead it looks to me like their bodies mirror each other's rhythm. So maybe that's a way of silent talking.

I don't know how or when the wedding grew into something stressful. It just gradually evolved into something that there isn't a spreadsheet big enough in the world to contain. Sometimes I think it's what I want and sometimes think it isn't, and Brendan just seems to go along with whatever's on the table as long as he doesn't have to get involved, and that means all the burden of decision-making rests on me. And that's starting to take some of the pleasure out of it. So perhaps this running on his own carries more meaning than he's willing to admit.

Brendan

I do the warm-down walk with Angela but feel I'd have liked to run for longer and further. Pauline tells us we've done well, that she can see by looking at us that we're stayers, that we aren't going to drop out when the nights get colder and our warm homes beg us not to leave them. She tells us too that she's sure we have what she calls the stickability necessary to complete the nine weeks. Then, when the session is over, Angela and I go our separate ways. I'm working night shifts so there'll just be time to take a shower and grab a bite to eat before I'm due on the wards.

After the running my body feels lighter even though sometimes my brain feels as if it's got more thoughts crowding in on it, but my work needs me to be clear-headed so I always pause a minute or so before going in and try to get my focus sharp. The nature of the work always demands your full attention and the problems of the people you encounter soon relegate your own preoccupations to the realm of the trivial.

As always when I come on duty, I call in the side ward where Judith has been moved. She hasn't long left. She's being transferred to a hospice soon. It hurts me to see her, a woman still young withered away like an autumn leaf, but it's a hurt I never reveal to her, and she's someone still with all her inner life seemingly unaltered. So she's resolute, always able to find something to laugh about. When I enter she opens her eyes and asks me how my running went and after I tell her I ran like the wind, she says, 'More like Forrest Gump.' I fix her sheets and even though I want to take her hand I don't but just busy about the room. As I'm about to leave she says she's getting married and I'm invited. I think it's the morphine talking and, when I glance back at her, her eyes close as she falls into sleep.

In the morning, after my shift is over and the city is only beginning to stir into life, I run on my own. It's my private time and I don't tell Angela about it. Try to let only music fill my head.

Yana

I've always tried to run. Even during the war as it came creeping ever closer, and in the camp in Lebanon, running down the tented alleyways and out to the edges of our confinement. When I was young my family told me that they disapproved, that it wasn't seemly for their daughter to be in constant motion as if she was fleeing from some bad thing they had done to her. But after so many bad things have happened for real, they have come to accept it. And perhaps they think that, in times of troubles such as ours, being able to run is no bad thing, that it has its uses.

Running under the sharpest of suns, even running through the first snows to smother the camp, my course tracked by the frozen prints left in my wake. Running despite the children who at first laughed at me, then occasionally tried to follow, as if I knew where there was some secret store of food, some better place that existed just beyond the fixed parameters of their world. I've never tried to explain it to anyone, but I know that it is in motion that I feel safest and most happy. That it's when my body feels as if it belongs to me and not someone else's expectation of who I should be. And when everything else has been taken from us – our home and livelihood, my oldest brother – this sensation that flows through me remains mine alone. In every stride is always the unspoken hope that I am moving to some better place for my family to follow. So it's as if I'm running ahead, scouting out our future days, searching for where we can be together, safely sleep through the night without starting awake at the slightest sound. Not anticipate the terror of the bombs falling before they've been launched. Not scurrying through the ruins looking for friends and family, not sitting in candlelit basements waiting for the help that never comes. Sometimes too I secretly think that if I run far and fast enough it will bring me to Masud who gave himself to the resistance, even though I know he is dead, his body scattered to the wind so there was nothing left to bury.

The soles of my trainers grew so thin it felt as if I was running in bare feet and when traversing the baked and rutted pathways my feet kicked up little spurts of red-coloured dust. Now I have new trainers. Now we are safe. But safe in a place that I didn't really know existed and which every day tells me that it isn't my home. Here with my father and mother and my little brother Issam who each night asks when we shall return and will Masud be waiting for us. We will try to make our new life in this place but never give up the hope of going back when the scars of war have healed, when things are rebuilt. And we're here as part of what is called the Vulnerable Persons Relocation Scheme, given a charity for which we are grateful, but it was war that made us vulnerable, not as a result of any actions of ours. And we have come from having a small restaurant and bakery business, of having the respect of our neighbours and society as a whole, to a new world based on this charity. But also to a world where there is sometimes resentment.

Everything conspires to remind us that we are outsiders – both the well-meaning people who are energetically kind and constantly welcoming, and those who stare with suspicion or make personal comments to each other which my English is good enough to understand, even though the accent I hear is so different to the one I am familiar with.

But it is the sky and sun under which I run in this my new home that are the most inescapable reminders. The sun is mostly absent or lurking behind clouds like someone secretive who wants to spy on the world below. And the sky seems to be a remote memory of the one under which I ran so often, with all its intensity of colour leached away so that it resembles some faded rag of a flag, a wind-blown tattered memory of its former self.

I know it is the hijab that attracts attention when I run, even though it is part of me and what I believe. They look at it as if it is a mystery to them and, in a way I don't understand, some see it as disrespectful to them, to whatever it is they believe in. There are some who have greeted my passing with shouts, calling names, and one man even offering an insult that suggested he thought I came from Pakistan. That is why I mostly run in the early morning along the towpath where the only people I meet are the occasional dog-walker and other runners. And I like the river, the light slowly stirring it into life and the trees that border it, the clean crispness of the air. Sometimes too I am able to think of Masud without it opening the wound inside again, remembering the early-morning visits to the market where he would buy falafel for us from a stall and which we'd eat sitting on the grass in the local park. Afterwards we would fly a kite – one that Masud would have made himself, and I wondered how such strong hands could make something so light. And of course he'd tease me by saying if I didn't hold the string tightly, the kite would lift me high in the air and he'd have to tell our mother that I'd been carried far away.

There are birds that sing along the riverbank and once I saw two swans. And how I like to think of Masud in these moments is as a kite that lifts his broken body back into the light, back into life. Lets him breathe once more the purest air and feel the sun warm his face so he's able to give me his smile again, tell me that everything will be all right. The water is glazed by the light so that it might mirror my reflection if I were to stop and stare into it. But its current is slow-moving, dreamlike, and I need to keep moving, keep running until I arrive at somewhere other than where I am.

I prefer to run on my own, to run in silence without the distraction of music or conversation, so joining the group is not what I wanted to do but it has been offered with such enthusiasm by the person who is charged with looking after us that I couldn't refuse. And everyone is friendly but I want to run, run until I am empty of the sharp-edged thoughts that plague me, run until I am able to remember the good things that go to make a home and gave me a place in the world other than the one allocated to the vulnerable. Not intersperse it with walking, not interrupt it with talking. So in this fourth week running for only five minutes before walking again feels like a kind of waste, a waste of the breath in my lungs, of the dreams in my head and the future I am desperate to reach.

But there is no evading Pauline, who for a minute runs beside me to see how I am getting on, tells me that I have a good style and then asks me how I find my new home.

'It's very nice,' I say. 'The people are very nice.'

The words trip off my tongue because I have used them so many times. It's what I say, and there is at least some truth in it so I don't feel guilty. And I know already it's what people like to hear. That it makes them feel good about themselves and where they live. But when I speak the words I can't always stop myself seeing again a blue sky, feel the taut string of a kite dancing on the lightest of breezes and taste a warm spice on my tongue. But I know too that I dream of something that only exists in memory and at night before I sleep I comfort myself with the thought that I have escaped a city ravaged and broken, its walls tumbled into dust. A place where my life and that of my family hung in a precarious balance.

As I force myself into the final walk of the session, I glance at the rest of the group and can't help wondering how many of them would have survived the journey out of Syria and across the border. A journey in which some of the very old and very young died on the way. A journey too that we had to make with only what we could carry and which ended up taking all our money to secure safe passage. In the sprawling camp I felt like a small grain of sand in the face of so many, the numbers swelling by the day, and where there was no possibility of privacy except inside my own head, when I've always been a private person, happy to be on my own. When things were really bad my father talked of attempting a sea crossing, but our mother's objections and the absence of funds to finance it saw his idea come to nothing.

Once the session is finished we stand in a half-circle and wait for Pauline to address us. I look at Maurice who walks with his hands on his hips and whose face is the colour of the red dust my feet once kicked up, at the couple who seem to be arguing quietly and at Cathy the woman who sometimes tries to talk to me, as Pauline tells us how well we're doing, that we're almost halfway there but that we need to be ready for Week Five so we must complete our independent run. She makes us give ourselves a round of applause before saying she'll see us next week.

The nights are really drawing in is what I hear people share with each other as we begin to disperse. I'm not sure what they mean. I am used only to the simplicity of two seasons – long hot summers and mild wet winters – but here everything is more complicated, unpredictable like a person who wears a different set of clothes every day. And there are times when I yearn for the sun to warm me, for it to seep into my skin and warm my very bones. But it too often feels like a stranger, someone who only begrudgingly acknowledges my existence, and as I walk home I understand that the days are heading into winter and know that this will be the time the light begins to die. That this is what is called the drawing in. Already the leaves on the trees along the river have turned brown and red and the water is slowly losing its sheen, so some days it looks like the colour of broken earthenware.

My eyes turn to the restaurants and fast-food shops as I walk. It is a city that is always eating and that is a good thing because both my mother and father are good cooks, and already they are talking about the possibility of having their own business once more, of making the food that has its origins in Syria. But how do they even start when there are so many obstacles in their way? I don't know the answer to this and do not want to see my parents stumble into the bitterness of another disappointment.

But no hurt will ever be as great or as lasting as the loss of Masud. And there's something I've never told them and which I know I never can. On the night before he secretly left, Masud came to my room just as I was falling into sleep and told me of his plan. He couldn't tell our parents because he knew they would try and stop him. There were so many things I wanted to say but he put his finger across my lips, briefly smoothed my hair and then he was gone into the night's darkness. Gone forever and if I had told my parents then maybe he would still be alive, be with us in our new home. It feels as if the world itself is suddenly drawing in, the light dying, and because there is nothing else I can offer in resistance, I start to run.

Maurice

It's the one I've been dreading. Week Five. By the
end of this we're supposed to run for twenty
minutes. Twenty minutes! A big jump from previous weeks. But I'm going to give it a go and my
running style is changing. I'm never going to be
able to stride out like Brendan, or Ciara who's
aiming to be a firefighter and who looks as if she's
already hoping for some blazing inferno to rush
into, but I'm not doing so much sideways moving
any more. I've developed what might be called
a soft-shoe shuffle, finding a pace that allows me
to keep going even though that blazing inferno
Ciara's looking for sometimes feels as if it's in my
chest. I've still not got enough surplus breath to
contribute much to the conversation that Cathy
likes to engage me in – I can't make up my mind
about her. Is she a good person or a bit of a busy-
body? She's a bit of a shuffler too, so we generally

end up running together, and she's definitely an organiser because she's arranged for a small group of us to combine on our independent run. There's no escaping her even if I wanted to.

A twenty-minute run and it's raining tonight. A fine rain that sifts down from a gloomy sky then grows gradually stronger. It's not a good omen. And suddenly I'm fearful that I'm going to humiliate myself, that I'm going to pull up on the hard shoulder of life with a clapped-out engine while everyone else motors past. The nights are drawing in and I pass a long-since-plundered horse chestnut tree, the grass below littered with discarded spiked shells. I have a sudden impulse to feign an injury – a pulled muscle, a sprained ankle – but I look at Pauline and think she's not going to accept a forged sick note and I know that I like her too much to lie to her. So after our five-minute brisk walk, off we set and yes, it's not about how fast we go but keeping going and in fact Pauline's urging everyone to slow down, to find a rhythm. Mina liked to dance but I never really had much sense of rhythm so I was mostly a kind of hand-holder, or a human maypole, while she gyrated around me and I'm truly sorry she didn't get to do 'Dancing in the Dark' with Bruce Springsteen. Sorry she didn't get to her post-retirement dance with life. Sometimes I've thought of visiting the places that were on our list but the idea of going alone holds no pleasure for me: every moment would be filled with the knowledge that she's not here any more. It's hard being one person after being two, and one of the many ways I miss her is that there's no one to give me advice on our daughter Rachel, no one to hold me back, no one to push me forward as situations demand.

I haven't seen Rachel and Ellie in three weeks. Well, that's not exactly true because while she hasn't called in that length of time, I have caught glimpses of her. Never on our small group run that takes us past her house, but when she's walking Ellie to the swimming pool or doing her weekly shop. And the phrase 'caught a glimpse' suggests something fortuitous, a happy coincidence, when the truth is I've started to try and anticipate where I might be likely to catch sight of her. So I park up the car and sit like some detective, except I guess most detectives don't drink tea from a flask while they're listening to 'Darkness on the Edge of Town' as they keep their suspect under surveillance, and it's not a suspect I'm watching out for but my own daughter, my own child. I don't believe in telepathic bonds or anything like that but I increasingly feel that things aren't right. I sense it in the way she walks, the way she holds Ellie's hand like the child is a kite that's going to be suddenly swept into the air when the first breeze blows. And if I don't look out for them both, I know I can never let myself think of Mina without bringing a sense of shame to her memory.

She never recovered consciousness after the car crash and, when I remember the hours I sat beside her hospital bed, I sometimes try to avoid that moment when they turned off the life-support system by imagining the things she would have said to me if she'd been able. And right after she'd told me to take proper care of myself, she would have made me promise to look out for Rachel and Ellie.

The rain is stronger now and I'm glad because I hope it might help cool my engine that is in danger of overheating. It feels as if there's something in my chest wanting to break out and, as Cathy burbles on about some book she's reading, I think that I'm about to re-enact a scene from *Alien* and a grotesque mutation is going to burst out. But maybe it's only my heart, my heart that feels as if it's going into overdrive as it pumps frantically while my lungs send out an SOS for more oxygen.

'All right, Maurice? You're doing great. Keep your posture upright – it holds your lungs open,' Pauline says.

'Please, sir, I have a stitch. Can I go and get changed?' are the actual words forming in my head in the voice of a young boy who's wearing nylon shorts and on one of those muddy cross-country runs so beloved by PE teachers. Instead I say, 'Doing OK, Pauline.'

But something is happening to time because Pauline is telling us we've completed ten minutes when she should be telling us that there's only a minute left. That we're halfway there when I want to hear that we're about to finish. And Cathy's not chirping in my ear any more, so she must be feeling it too. I glance at her and her face is forward-looking and glazed by the rain. It makes her seem a little saintly and I think she'd be pleased if I told her that, but it's not the type of thing you can say and I haven't any breath to spare.

Puddles are forming on the path but they're not deep enough for me to waste energy going around so I just plough through, skittering little diamond droplets of water about both our ankles. And the big question at the heart of this is: when does it get easier? When does it stop hurting? I'm hoping it's soon because I can't go much further. And I'd be more than happy to do a Captain Oates and for the good of everyone say that I'm just going outside and may be some time. Except I am outside and, as we pass the naked horse chestnut tree again, I've started to feel like one of those hollow shells with all my insides plucked out.

Mark didn't even come to Mina's funeral and that suited me fine. He was in Scotland, supposedly seeing some mate, and he never made it back. So it was me and Rachel sitting in the front pew and there was a moment when we held hands but it wasn't long enough. And while I sat in the church that our family only frequents for christenings, weddings and funerals, I thought how good it would have been to walk my daughter down that same aisle and see her marry some guy who's going to love her, look after her. Make her happy. But maybe that's what's wrong with life – we're all needing someone to make us happy as if we can't ever achieve it by ourselves. And if we're lucky or unlucky enough to find someone, what happens when they're not there any more?

I don't know if it's because I'm seeing her from a distance that Rachel looks thinner, and even though she once took pride in her appearance, spending a small fortune on clothes and make-up, now she looks a little throughother. A little gaunt. And one morning after she had left Ellie off at nursery, she spent about an hour sitting in the park as if she didn't want to go home. I thought of suddenly appearing but bottled it, telling myself that I didn't want to risk her knowing that I was watching out for her. It's the same park where I used to take her as a child. She liked the swings best, always wanting you to push her higher. And that's how I like to think of her — not sitting alone on a park bench, looking cold and thin, but on a swing, swinging out over the city, swinging so high it feels like she's flying over the roofs of the terraced streets and even over the shipyard cranes.

The rain is really heavy now but we have five more minutes to go. I start to hope for a 'rain stops play' announcement over some invisible tannoy, but under an increasingly sullen sky there's only the wet slap of feet. All day long I see five minutes pass in the blink of an eye and now every minute, every microsecond, is an eternity in itself, the hands of Pauline's stopwatch seemingly trapped in permanent and malevolent slow motion. In my delirium a song starts in my head and I silently sing it with rising desperation and it's 'Come On

Eileen' except on its own internal loop it becomes 'Come on, Pauline. Come on, Pauline. Blow that bloody whistle.'

And then finally it goes and we're all supposed to fall into a brisk walk, but I've found a wooden post to embrace and it feels like the only thing keeping me upright. I'm hunched over it, holding the top of it with both hands, trying to find a breath that doesn't feel like it's travelled from the furthest regions of outer space. This must be what it's like to be in the death zone on Everest where the air is so thin it makes a single step a monumental effort. And then I'm conscious of hands patting me on the back and people are saying 'Well done' and it's a bit of a shock because the only intimacy I associate with group physical activity is the snap of a wet towel in a school changing room. 'Well done, Maurice,' the voices say and hands are still patting me even though I can't see whose they are because my face is pushed up into the post as if I'm about to kiss it. At first I don't want to let go of it in case I fall over and then Pauline's encouraging me to loosen my hold, to straighten myself and get some air in my empty lungs. And I'm touched. Touched in so many ways that I can't begin to explain.

'Well done, Maurice, you did it,' she says and I try to smile but say nothing in reply because I know that if I am to speak, I shall start to cry and that's not a good look for a man of my age who's wearing an extra-large royal-blue Fusion Pro quick-dry long-sleeve half-zip running top and a pair of also extra-large tracksuit bottoms. And it's not because I have reverted to childhood, conscious that my feet are wet, or that I have a damp bottom where the rain has sluiced down off my top. It's because I hear Mina telling me that I have to look after myself and have to look after Rachel and Ellie, and because while I'm trying to do the first of these, I don't know how to do the second. Don't know how to care for our daughter and grandchild, except to watch over them and keep myself ready. And then as everyone begins to walk ahead, I linger behind until, despite my best efforts, a few tears start. I wipe them clear, hoping that if anyone turns round, they'll think it's only the rain. Only a man wiping away the rain.

Cathy

Even though I said I'm not actively looking for a partner, and for the minute at least am concentrating on running this 5K, it doesn't stop me thinking about men. Martina in the library tried online dating a year ago and ended up with a man sending her a photograph of a body part that she really didn't want to see. Before she blocked him she sent him a message saying she'd prefer to see an image of his brain, but as that was probably as small as his – well, you-know-what – she'd have to invest in a magnifying glass. It made us laugh over morning coffee, but setting aside those suitors whose behaviour and motivations categorically and eternally debar them from serious consideration, I worry about men who are good at pretending to be one thing when they're really something else. And I worry about finding out the truth when things have gone too far and you're vulnerable, enmeshed in some too-plausible spider's web.

Because although Henry my husband had probably stopped loving me a long time before he left, I hadn't realised. That's partly my fault, taking things for granted, just getting on with life and thinking everything will look after itself. And there's a trust issue involved for me now as well, because he'd been having a relationship with his work colleague and I never suspected. Maybe that makes me naive – I don't know. But it does make you think about what type of man you want, and I'm better at knowing what I don't want rather than what I do. So I don't want any Heathcliffs – none of that brooding darkness with a propensity for violence; nor a Mr Rochester with some secret lurking in the attic. And I never really found the television Darcy attractive either, not even after his wet-shirt episode, because he's like those men who always have a ready-made apology for how they behave and need so much re-engineering to help them become someone you'd want to spend your life with.

But what do I want? Well, independent means, for a start. I don't intend sharing my meagre pension with anyone, especially now that the government has moved the retirement age in the hope that more of us will die before we get back some of the money we've contributed to the Exchequer. This is when I start to struggle with the words for what I want and if I say a sense of moral responsibility, then it makes people think I'm looking for some Victorian vicar in a frock coat. But yes, someone who's able to care. Care about me, care about others, who has a clear vision of what's right and doesn't need someone to constantly point out what's wrong. But I don't know how you construct any of this into a personal profile you post online. So for the moment at least I'm focusing only on completing this running programme, even though I struggled with the twenty-minute run last week and my shins are starting to complain. Following Pauline's advice, I've bought a couple of pairs of compression socks – they're supposed to increase the oxygen supply to the muscles and improve circulation. When I told Martina about them, she said I should wear one on my head.

I don't know if it's part of my called-back-to-life feeling after my recent health scare, but aside from my shins I'm increasingly conscious of the physical benefits of my five weeks of running. I've a fuller appetite and I'm sleeping better too, no longer waking up at the first break of light slithering into the room through curtains that have never been heavy enough to prevent its entry. And it's offered some counterbalance to my worries about my daughter Zara who's pregnant with her second child and frightened that it will prove as difficult as her previous ones. Our conversations on Skype are still awkward, trying to construct chat round the things that we know aren't important, almost as if, were we to venture into the things that really matter, somehow our connection will get lost and into that absence will flow all the thousands of miles that separate us.

And, despite the positive feelings about my own body, I'm still checking it religiously and think that when you've been granted a reprieve you should make the most of the future given back to you.

I've been thinking too about how so many of us lose our children. Lose them to faraway countries and better jobs, to what they see as improved opportunities. They go off at eighteen to get educated and we're proud of them, but then most of them don't come back. Perhaps it's just because other places are able to offer more of the things they want. Perhaps it's because when they look back at where they were born, it seems a small place, eternally locked into its ancient feuds and tribal bitterness, a place where prejudice is still allowed to legislate how people should live. Change is coming but it comes too slow for the impatience of youth. And for generations this whole island has seen its children emigrate, and while it's true that it's easier nowadays to stay in touch through FaceTime and Skype, through all the benefits of technology, it doesn't make it any easier in your heart. You can't reach out your arms into the screen, can't touch the body of your child, can't talk to them without feeling like you're performing in some way, with everything stilted and awkward. Everything just on the surface. Nothing ever below. Putting on a brave face. Not being able to tell your only child about your health scare, not being able to share sadness.

Hoping too that tragedy never blurs the images on the screen, because there is no language able to deal with that. Maurice has never spoken of his wife but a few days ago someone told me about the accident. It came as a bit of a shock. I always thought there was a sadness about him and when he runs it's as if he's carrying some burden that goes beyond his surplus weight. I think he's probably let himself go a bit and that's understandable in some ways after a tragedy like that. But all credit to him for getting himself up and running, and the price stickers finally fell off his trainers during that night we ran in the rain. And while running in the rain might hold some kind of resonance for romantics, I didn't find any in damp knickers and wet feet, my hair plastered to my skull like rats' tails. The only pleasure was a post-run long soak in a hot bath accompanied by candles and a gin and tonic.

It's a nice bunch of people in the running group and I've had a chat with almost all of them now, usually when we're waiting around about to start or when we pair up while walking. Women are able to tell each other lots of things, even though it's not long since they were complete strangers. So I know about some of Angela's wedding plans, her problems with finding the right dress and what she thought of Meghan Markle's – a bit plain was her verdict; about Maureen's mother who has the beginnings of dementia; and Elise the classroom assistant who by all accounts needs to have the patience of a saint; and about Zofia whose cleaning business now employs five people but who's going back to Poland if Brexit makes things too difficult. Only Yana is a closed book, not just because she holds herself a little apart, but mostly because she runs so fast, always striding purposefully out as if she's no time to waste in getting to wherever it is she wants to go.

A closed book that unexpectedly opens some of its pages. On a slow day before the schoolkids arrive and after the unemployed have left, she comes into the library. She recognises me, but doesn't say anything to reveal that recognition, and she wants to join. She doesn't have any form of identification new members are supposed to have, but I bend the rules and register her. I give her a little tour, show her how to sign into the computers, and all the time I'm thinking of saying something about our running, but perhaps the fact that I don't is the reason she eventually asks me if I'm enjoying the sessions. When I tell her I found Week Five hard she smiles, because I think it didn't represent a challenge for her, but then she says I'm doing well. That it will get easier.

I say that perhaps I'm too old for it and she shakes her head and tells me I'm not old and then, although it might seem rude, I ask her age and she tells me nineteen and after I ask about her family I mention my daughter in Australia and reveal that I'm a grandmother. She asks me if I miss her and when I say yes, I ask her how she's settling into her new home. But even though she says the right things I see there's a sadness in her eyes, that part of her is looking back at things she's unable to talk about, so I don't push her and after our own troubles we're experts at sidestepping the consequences of trauma by not talking about it.

She tells me that her family are bakers and she wants to use a computer to see if there might be restaurants in the city that would be interested in using some of the food they could produce, of how they hope to find premises where they could cook and bake. I don't know for sure but I say there might be government help with start-up grants for small businesses and stuff like that. That I'll make some enquiries, ask a few people who might know. As soon as I've said it I start to worry that I've conjured some hope of help that I won't be able to deliver. But I know I'll try.

Just as I'm going to try on this, our Week Six independent run, where we have to walk for five minutes, run for ten, then walk for three followed by a final ten-minute run. It doesn't sound too bad when you say it like that, so I try not to think about the twenty-five-minute run with which we're supposed to finish the week. I had asked Yana if she'd like to join our small group, but she said she preferred to run early morning along the river.

Perhaps I'm conscious of her choice of running route and that's why I suggest that we change our normal circuit and follow the river before looping back to our starting point. It seems a good call. Only Maurice looks a little disappointed, probably because we won't be running past his daughter's house, but he doesn't say anything and so we set off following the Lagan's slow curve to where it will eventually end in the Lough. The air tingles crisp and clean and a single oarsman rows a smooth furrow through the water, his steady rhythm an example to all of us. We mostly have the path to ourselves, apart from the occasional cyclists who politely ring their bells to warn they're going to overtake.

It's when we've just finished our first ten-minute run that we see them. Thousands and thousands of starlings, a great shifting and pulsing cloud churning and shading the sky, twisting and turning in on itself. We stand transfixed and watch, momentarily forgetting about our second run. Someone says it's a pity we can't move like that, and Brian starts to give some scientific explanation, but then I hear nothing more except a kind of murmuration in the heart, because what I'm seeing is the thousands of our sweet-souled children set in flight and I want to reach out my hand to them to wave them home, or wherever the home is that brings them happiness.

'Are you all right?' Maurice asks.

'Yes, thanks, Maurice. Just having a moment.'

'You look sad,' he says.

'Give me a hug, Maurice,' I tell him.

Then he does and after the briefest of touches we set out on our final run.

Brendan and Angela

I didn't expect to see him waiting there. I'd just come off shift to find Angela's father Aidan standing beside my car, giving it the once-over, a kind of visual MOT, and I could tell from his expression, and the way his fingers traced the dent in the door where I had an argument with a car-park bollard, that he was mentally failing it. But as soon as he saw me it was all bonhomie and best-mates stuff, and supposedly he thought it a good idea that we hang out a little and shoot the breeze. But he's not good at subtlety, so before I could even produce my keys he was offering me a new car – well, one of his cast-offs actually – something he obviously thought more suitable for his future son-in-law to be seen around town in. And as I politely declined I suspected we had reached that point in dramas where concerned fathers offer lowlifes a substantial financial inducement to drop any pretence of love for their daughter and depart forthwith. I glanced at the pocket of his coat because I imagined that he was no stranger to bunging people wads of money in brown paper bags in car parks. And there were rumours doing the rounds that he wasn't entirely detached from some of the ongoing NAMA property scandal, but he also had a reputation for having all his business interests Teflon coated.

But if a brown paper bag was going to emerge from a pocket, there was no sign of it yet and instead his empty hand rested lightly on my shoulder for a second while he invited me for something to eat, telling me it was important we got to know each other better before the big day. I couldn't refuse and so we ended up in a city-centre restaurant where the staff knew him by name, saw that we got a suitably appropriate table and served his usual drink before he'd even ordered it. After a few cursory questions about work and how the running was going, he launched into a mini biography of himself whose purpose was to let me know that he was a self-made man, that he'd started out with nothing and grafted to make something of himself. It got most embarrassing when he said he grew up in a house just like the one my parents still lived in, with the unspoken implication that if only they had grafted as hard as he did then the golden prizes would have been theirs.

I did a lot of non-committal nodding and waited for the brown paper bag to be pushed across the table. It came between the main and dessert, prefaced by a question about where I saw myself in ten years' time, and after I had avoided any meaningful response, he offered me a job. An opportunity had come for him to acquire a certain city-wide property portfolio and he thought that Angela and I would be the ideal people to manage it. I had no idea what managing a property portfolio entailed and wasn't interested in finding out, but before I was allowed to reply he insisted that I think about it, give it suitable consideration and talk to Angela before coming back with an answer.

So my fate was not to be dispatched from the family but to be incorporated in it. The end result felt the same. I wondered if Angela had known about this offer in advance of it sliding across the table. The following night, as we turn up for our second group running session of the week, I don't say anything and wait to see if she'll raise it, but she says nothing and seems focused only on completing her run. At first I try to run with her, but find it difficult to keep to her pace, and she must realise this because she tells me to go on ahead and so I leave her, fall into my own rhythm. Afterwards I tell her that she's done well, that I know she's going to make the final run, and we hug briefly. When she tells me there must be an easier way, I say I know it's hard but she's doing great and it'll be worth it in the end. But I don't say anything about the job, nor do I tell her that after the programme finishes I'm going to keep on running, that I run each morning before work. That it's doing something good for both my body and my head.

I don't have to think much about Aidan's offer – I already have two families, the one that brought me into the world and the one I work in every day, so I've no need of another. When I'm back on the wards I'm aware of a bit of a commotion in Judith's room and after I go to see what's going on, I find a group of people standing round her bed and realise she *is* actually getting married, that it wasn't the morphine talking. She signals me in and I see that she has a little scarf of white lace round her neck and matching lace gloves on her hands – it's the closest her wasted body can come to wearing a wedding dress – and the groom, her partner of fifteen years, wears a dark suit and white shirt with a spray on his lapel. It's a humanist service and after they do the vows her two sisters sing a cappella. I stand in the corner and try to hold it together like I'm supposed to do and after the ceremony is finished Judith calls me over and asks if I'm not going to give the bride a kiss. So I bend down and lightly kiss her hollow cheek, shake hands with the groom and then leave them to their precious time together.

But I can't get it out of my head. And that weekend, when we go to stay in an apartment on the north coast owned by Angela's parents, the images press themselves into my consciousness. And they're accompanied by thoughts about the unpredictability of life, the preciousness of time shared and most of all what real love looks like. How it doesn't need anything, not a single thing, except what exists between two people.

On Saturday morning I wake early and then ease Angela awake, tell her that we need to go for a run on the beach. She asks if I'm crazy, offers me an alternative form of exercise, but I tell her we have to run and I think she can see that it's important to me so she gets up and we both put on our running gear. We walk through the dunes to the beach, the marram grass sharp against our hands. The sky is full of the winter's morning light stretching cloudlessly over the calmness of the sea, the beach almost empty with the tide out and the sand shining in a kind of diamond brightness. We walk towards the water through soft rucks of sand to reach where it's firmer underfoot and look out towards the horizon.

'It's beautiful,' she says and then we stand in silence.

A little trill of white-edged water ripples close to our feet, making me think of the white lace that served for a wedding dress and how in that moment it seemed more beautiful than the most expensive creation. How every moment I spent in that side room felt more real to me than just about anything else I've ever experienced. And I've slowly come to a decision. A decision about the wedding, about Angela, about if we have a future together or not. It's simple in a way, because it all comes down to one thing, and that's whether she's going to try and persuade me to work for her father. If she does then I know we'll never have an independent life, always be in the shadow of someone else, and that we can't be enough for each other purely on our own. So I'm nervous as we turn and start to do our walk as a warm-up. Frightened that we've finally reached this moment because, despite the certainty of our synchronised steps, I'm unsure of where they're taking us.

The five minutes of walking seem to last an eternity and I check the phone app to see if it's actually working. Then we start to run and I'm keeping it at a really gentle pace, even getting her to slow down as we aim for the end of the beach and the stone pier that stretches into the sea. Our faces are splashed clean by the freshness of the air and for a second it feels like we're inhaling the right type of drug. Sometimes a little break of water runs towards us and she squeals as we have to veer further up the beach out of its reach. Perhaps the tide is starting to come in. Then a few seconds later I feel her hand plucking at my arm, signalling me to stop, and I think there's something wrong but she wants us to take our trainers off so we leave them further up the beach and start to run again at the water's edge, our feet splashing up little glitters of water. In the morning light without a stitch of make-up, she looks beautiful and I think that my heart will break if I am faced with the truth that what we have isn't going to work. So, hard as it is, I try to stay in the preciousness of these few moments, don't want us ever to reach the end of the beach. And she's running well, displaying the determination she brings to everything she does, even if occasionally she's wincing at the coldness of the water, water that's clean and clear so we can see the wavy ridges of sand that we feel on the soles of our feet.

Far out to sea, like a smudge on the horizon, lurks the motionless shadow of a tanker and sometimes our splashes are accompanied by the screeches of gulls in a discordant duet. But we run on and, although I don't want it, the stone pier is getting closer. Getting closer with every step, no matter how I try to slow our pace. And then unexpectedly she's pushing on faster, determined to beat me, and I'm happy to let her, happy to trail in her splashing wake. So she's waiting for me at the base of the pier, sitting on one of the black rocks that have been placed there as a breakwater.

'What's keeping you, slowcoach?' she teases.

I don't answer, because I don't know how to start, but somehow instinctively she seems to sense what's in my head and says that we should talk. So I sit beside her on the rock and we stare again out to sea, neither of us sure how to begin.

Eventually she asks, 'What are you going to do about my dad's offer of a job?'

'I'm going to refuse,' I tell her and study her face intently to see her reaction.

There's a pause and then she says, 'That's good. Glad you didn't let me down. I told him you wouldn't accept.'

When I ask her if she's sure, she tells me that she is, that it would never work. And I'm so happy, so relieved, that everything suddenly tumbles out about the wedding, about what I had witnessed with Judith, and I don't know if any of it even makes sense but she's nodding and that makes me bolder and I hear myself yielding to the most unexpected but powerful of impulses, saying, 'Let's get married here on the beach. You have to apply for a licence but others have done it. Look at it – it's really beautiful. Some chairs, a bit of bunting, a little table for the registrar, some music.' And she doesn't start to scream, in fact she starts to laugh then asks, 'And after?'

'Hire the hall in the community centre, get some caterers in. We'll let your dad look after that if he wants.'

'How long have you been planning this?' she asks, but she's still got a smile on her face. Then she tells me that she'll think about it, think about it while we're running back along the beach to where we left our shoes, and then before I get a chance to reply she sets off, her feet kicking up fantails of sparkled light.

Yana

On the morning when our parents discovered Masud had gone, I pretended ignorance of his whereabouts. It hurt me to deceive them but I felt I had no choice. They found out soon enough after a series of phone calls revealed that he had left with some of his friends. I can't think of that morning without hearing the wails of my mother, seeing once more her shaking hands above her head, my father's frantic phone calls to relatives and people in authority to try and discover where he might be, so that he could go and bring him home, bring their firstborn son home to the safety of his family. But they never saw him again and spoke to him only once more, the week before they learned of his death – in a phone call made difficult by an intermittent signal. Killed in an air strike, killed along with three of his friends who had left with him.

The cold morning air presses tightly against my face almost as if I'm wearing it like a mask. I have a pair of woollen gloves to keep my hands warm. A delicate tracery of spiders' webs trembles in the hedgerow in the breeze. The river seems almost motionless, as if uncertain about which way it should flow. On its surface float little spirals of fallen leaves. It feels as if the world is contracting into itself, shedding what it doesn't need in preparation for the worst of the winter that's coming. It snowed in the camp in Lebanon, adding to the misery, layering the tents and improvised dwellings with an additional burden that made the world feel cruel. As if it hadn't given them enough suffering already. Two days of heavy snow and the diesel fuel needed to fire the oil burners running out. It felt as if the cold had simply bypassed my skin and seeped into my bones.

Only the pace of my running stops me shivering at the memory. They have given me warm clothing for the cold days ahead, but sometimes it feels as if I am wearing what belongs to someone else, living another person's life. Living it but without the full knowledge or understanding of how it should be lived. Not understanding some of the expressions the people use, or the geography of the city, not able to anticipate the weather, and most of all never being fully at home inside myself. Sometimes it makes me feel like a stranger to the person I once was. Only the running is the same, a rhythm that links me seamlessly to who I was before and the world I have left. Masud used to tease me about it, saying it was a waste of valuable energy that could be used for other things. When I joined in the game and asked what other things he meant, he'd make up ridiculous things and tell me that if I connected myself to a dynamo I could generate electricity. Light up the darkness during the power cuts.

And there is something else that makes me not only feel like a stranger to myself but a stranger to others, because I can never tell anyone about some of the things I've seen. About the bodies in the rubble after the bombing, the fly-ridden bodies bloated and rotting in the sun that we passed along the road on the journey into Lebanon. The old and the newborn who died in the camp with the snow preventing their burial. The images are locked inside and have nowhere to go, flitting through my mind at unpredictable times like the shadows convulsed against the walls of the tent lit only by the oil-fired heater. Sometimes, when people look at me with ill-disguised curiosity, I think it's not because of the colour of my skin or what I'm wearing but because they can see some of those memories projected across my face in all their grotesque detail.

I know too that my attitude to people has changed and is marked by suspicion. There were stories of people who settled old scores by betraying their neighbours and then stole their property and possessions. And my family had been deceived by those who had taken money to drive us across the border and then never appeared. Left us standing for hours in the dusk, watching as bats pierced the dark skies, black pulses between the stars. Issam falling asleep in his mother's arms. The slow trudge back to our home, conscious with every step of our father's simmering anger and humiliation. The deception made more bitter, not easier, when we learned that others had been similarly deceived by the same people.

An old man on the towpath, walking a tiny dog, raises his cap to me as I run past. A female jogger says 'Hi' but I barely respond to either of them. Who can be trusted? Who is not motivated by greed or selfishness? How can I know for sure who wishes us well and who wishes us harm? Already

I am experiencing doubt about telling the woman in the library about my family – the woman in the running group called Cathy. What good can come of it? Better to keep things to myself, to run alone like this. To not look anyone in the eye and hold myself close to the edges of everything.

The river is stirred by the rising wind, with little eddies threading its surface and quivering the reeds that border the banks, their seeded heads leaning in as if whispering to each other. Some of the trees still cling to a few leaves that have reddened into a slow smoulder of fire. I've never seen trees with such a host of colours and don't want to think of their branches finally bare. And there are other secrets inside our home as well as the one I hide about knowing that Masud was going off to fight. Issam hasn't been told about his brother's death, the brother he idolised and about whom he speaks every day. My parents say he is too young to be told, that it will hinder him adapting to his new home, but sometimes when I argue that he needs to know I see the sadness in their eyes and understand that the telling, the putting it into the permanence of words, is too unbearably painful a prospect for them. But it means that every day we hear him ask when

Masud will join us, asking if he is minding our home for when we return.

And yet of all of us Issam has been the one who has fitted in most easily, loving his new school that has been good to him and provided him with new friends and new interests. He has started to play on the football team and learned new computer skills, got invited to other children's birthday parties. He's even been away on a school trip to an outdoor adventure centre. But it's obvious he misses Masud terribly, misses him as we all do. It is our mother who struggles most, not finding her language lessons easy, worrying about her extended family and friends with whom she has mostly lost contact. Not knowing how to mourn in a strange country, bereft of her son and without the comfort of the rituals that serve to salve grief. She treasures the few photographs she managed to carry with her on our hurried flight, clasping them like sacred objects. Hers is a journey into exile that has no sign of ending and some nights, when it's time for Issam to go to bed, she sings the old songs to him, as if she hopes they might filter into his dreams so he doesn't forget the land that once was ours.

Suddenly a dog starts towards me, barking until its owner pulls on its lead, and then the man says,

'Sorry, luv. Don't mind him. He wouldn't harm you. Just likes the sound of his own voice.' I run on, a little shaken, the moment giving me renewed speed as I seek to put distance between myself, the dog and its owner. And each step makes me feel something different on this morning, as if I'm not running further into my future, however uncertain that might be, but rather deeper into secrets and what is hidden.

It was something I was going to have to reveal before the spread of the war, but now, after everything that's happened, it's even more difficult because they rely on me, so perhaps it can never be shared with anyone. But I have known for a long time that I don't want to give the rest of my life to baking and the family business, that I can't contemplate the fixed parameters this offers. I have always been willing to help, to do the things that need to be done – no one can say I have ever been lazy or thought myself above the daily labour. But I can't give the rest of my life to the endless flare of oven heat and reddened hands, the kneading and making, the constantly selling something to others. What I want for myself isn't fully clear but I know I want to go to university, to learn new things, things that will be important in the years to come.

The only other person who knew what was in my head was Masud. He had encouraged me, told me to be like the kite we flew, to rise up above our confines and see the world beyond. But told me also that I could do this and still stay attached to my family, that there were deep bonds that could not be broken. I wanted to tell my parents when the time was right. But now there is no right time, because they need me more than ever, depend on my ability to speak the language. So while part of me knows that I have escaped from the terror, another part feels trapped in a future that is not the one I want.

The wind shivers some lingering leaves from the trees. One of them floats languidly down across my path. I stop and pick it up, stare at its burnt-ochre colouring, trace the leaf's veins with the tip of my finger. It seems cruel that in the moment it's most beautiful it comes closest to death. Sometimes I try to tell myself that Masud is not dead because no body was ever returned to us. That he might be hiding somewhere or taken prisoner, even that he made it safely over the border into Lebanon or Jordan. Although I know there is little chance of any of these hopes being true.

I start to walk. Suddenly running seems a deception, just a way of avoiding the realities that govern my existence. I slip the leaf into the pocket of my jeans. In the distance a plane sews a vapour trail through the sky. I wonder where it's going, then wonder too whether my restlessness will serve to make me a poor daughter, a poor sister to Issam, and stop me finding any sense of contentment in my new home. I remember the little birds in cages our elderly neighbour kept hanging from his garden wall and how he cried when he released them after the first wave of bombing. What happened to them? Did they take wing and find a safer home, or are they still in endless flight looking for some- where to build their nests?

I look again at the river, which now seems to have shaken itself into a deeper, fuller flow as if woken from its slumber; at the trees on either side of it beginning to bend and rustle as the wind sifts through them; and all the world seems stirred into sudden motion, a motion that I need to be part of. So I start to run again, remembering Masud's words and believing that it is the only way I know to light up the darkness.

Cathy

It's the first time I've seen Maurice with his clothes on. And he looks quite dapper in his Marks and Spencer way. The first time, in fact, I've seen any of my running colleagues in their ordinary clothes, apart from Yana who comes regularly to the library. Around my kitchen table sit Maurice, Brian, Zofia, Elise and Yana. I've brewed up a pot of tea and plated up some bought shortbread that I'm hoping they might think I've baked. Also on the table are lots of pamphlets, computer printouts and writing materials, so it's all businesslike. I'm happy to let Brian the accountant lead, as he has the most direct experience, although it's useful that Maurice knows his way round local government and still has good contacts. And while it's clear that Brian and Maurice have plenty of relevant knowledge, it's also evident that Zofia has the best practical experience of setting up a small business, seems to know the inside track and, despite not being here all that long, has an intimate insight into what's happening in the city.

Yana is understandably nervous but she accepts a cup of tea and a bit of shortbread that I suspect has been sitting in my cupboard slightly too long, which embarrasses me when I remember her family are bakers. At first Brian is explaining things and offering a way forward in a very simplified style, talking too slowly and deliberately, but as soon as Yana speaks and asks some pertinent questions, he seems to realise that he's not speaking to a child. He's going to help her family with a business plan, find the right agency, get the complicated forms filled in, and Maurice is going to help with the figures. And talking about figures, it's obvious he's lost weight, has confined himself to a single piece of shortbread, although that might be a judgement on its quality rather than his self-discipline. It's left a little sprinkling of sugar across his chest that I have to stop myself brushing off.

Zofia has contacts in the restaurant trade that she can sound out and also thinks she knows where there might be some premises that could be rented cheaply. My contribution is to make more tea. When I place the fresh pot on the table, Elise is floating the idea of online crowdfunding, but when it's explained to Yana she says her father couldn't accept it, couldn't accept any more charity than he's received already because he is a proud man. We try to explain there'd be lots of people out there who want to help, that it's not really charity, but she seems fixed in her opinion so we don't push it any further.

When the business part of the evening is finally over, our talk inevitably turns to our last week of running and the coming parkrun. We're chittering nervously, like children about to take our end-of-term exam, and I tell everyone that I've found the longer runs really hard and haven't managed one without having to walk a little. Elise and Maurice say they're the same but then I offer the hope that on the big day the crowd of people we'll be running amongst might give us the extra encouragement we need to complete it. Pauline has told us that we'll be fine, that she's going to run with us and it's not the time that's important, it's doing your best and finishing. And when we complete our run it isn't over, because we'll wait at the finishing line and encourage home every single one of our group. That's made me worry that I'll be the one keeping everyone waiting, that they'll have to send out a search party for me.

And then, as everyone starts to pack up, Yana stands and says that her father has invited us all to their home, that he'd like to meet us and say thanks. It will be two nights before our Saturday final run. I think we're all a bit surprised but it's not an invitation anyone wants to refuse. Before he goes Maurice asks me if I want a lift to Yana's parents' and I say yes, then forget myself and brush the white sugar beading off his jumper.

Yana's house is small but tidy and her parents greet us like we're long-lost family members. Her father speaks a little English but formally welcomes us through Yana's translation. Then he makes a joke about Yana running so much, telling us even as a young child she would disappear and the whole family would be out looking for her. Brian suggests they should have fitted her with a tracker but the joke gets lost in translation and then we're brought into the kitchen. On a table is a spread of vividly coloured sweets and pastries with a rich golden glaze, candies and sweetmeats. There is other food, some of it with intensely vibrant, spiced colours, and we ask Yana to talk us through it. She points to what she calls Aleppo pistachio, to shawarma with lamb, hummus, falafel, pitta bread and salad. We all instinctively pull out our phones and take pictures.

It all tastes delicious and makes us think that the city must have a place for food like this. And for perhaps the first time I begin to think that they could really make a go of things. Brian says it's just as well we have time to recover before our Saturday morning run, as he helps himself to a second portion of the falafel. Yana's parents look on with obvious pride, taking advantage of any moment's respite on our part to make new offerings. We also meet Yana's little brother Issam, who's a little shy at first but then chats about his school in good English flavoured with a local accent. Afterwards we drink strong but sweetened coffee.

On the journey home I ask Maurice if he's nervous about our big run and after he tells me that he is I realise that when it's finished we might not see each other or any of the others again. The thought saddens me but I don't know what might preserve the connections we've made and I ask him if he intends to stay with running. After a little thought he says he probably won't, although he's going to keep on with some sort of fitness programme but isn't sure what form it will take. He's seen some sort of tennis-style game called pickleball adver- tised in his leisure centre and he thinks he might give it a go. Then, staring resolutely ahead and with both his hands clenching the wheel tightly, he says that whatever happens he's not going back to the couch. I tell him even regular walking is good and that I've seen a brochure with some lovely-looking walking holidays – in the Swiss Alps, in Majorca and Croatia. As soon as I've said it I know how it sounds and so I try to backtrack by talking about Yana's family and the food we've just eaten.

But the moment when I should get out of the car passes. Suddenly there is a cascade of brightly coloured sparks in the night sky where someone has set off fireworks left over from Halloween. We both crane our necks to watch their slow cascade as they drift into nothingness. I go to say something about sparklers and toffee apples but before I can, Maurice, without taking his eyes off the night sky, tells me about his daughter Rachel and how worried he is about her. There are things I could say but I don't interrupt. And even when he's finished I don't offer easy advice, because it's complicated and I too am a little frightened. So we both sit silently in the car without any burst of illumination shooting across the dark sky, until I ask him if he'd like to come in for a coffee and he turns his head and looks at me, almost as if he's seeing me for the first time. He hesitates and thanks me, but then says he should be heading home, and I pat his arm twice and get out of the car.

I stand on the pavement watching as he drives away. None of us ever knows what secrets lie beneath the surface of other people's lives. That's something I've learned late in life and if anything should encourage us not to rush to judgement, it's that. And I understand now that look on his face when we did our run past his daughter's house, his uncertainty and his fear about what went on behind its closed door. I feel a wave of compassion for him, for his daughter and her child. And I think of my own daughter Zara in Australia and suddenly the miles that separate us don't seem the worst thing in the world, and only for the fact that by now she will be fast asleep, I'd speak to her and tell her that her mother loves her and everything will be all right.

On Saturday morning it's Pauline who's telling us that everything indeed will be all right. That we've been a great group and she's proud of us whatever happens. She reminds us again that we start the run and finish as a team, waiting at the end until every single one of us has crossed that line. Sometimes I think Pauline would be the best prime minister we could ever have, telling this nation what it needs to hear. The things that would make it better at this time when everyone seems to be pulling in different directions. I'm glad we've done a whip-round and bought her a bunch of flowers, a decent bouquet and not some last-minute one picked up on a garage forecourt.

It's the perfect day for it – cool and dry with the winter sun shining, if a little weakly – and I'm surprised by the huge number of people who've turned up. There's other groups like ours, some wearing matching colours, and individuals with watches on their wrists and whose lean limbs suggest they are practised runners. But there's all ages, right from the very young to the very old, and if truth be told, all shapes. One man is dressed as a crocodile and one as Spiderman. There's a couple who have T-shirts with a picture of a toddler on the front and underneath the words 'For Emily' with the all-too-brief dates of her life. And there's a presentation before the start when a man called Eamon, who we're told is eighty years of age, gets a special medal for competing in his hundredth run. As we clap him I wish for this morning at least he'd lend me some of his genes or whatever it is that enables him to do this.

We've all registered online in advance, so we will be given a finishing time even though, as Pauline says, for most of us that's not the crucial thing. Whatever happens now, I'm glad I've done it. And whether or not it's good for my body, including my complaining shins, the feeling of being part of something where no one is left out, and that has no motivation other than the common good, has to be worthwhile and, bizarre as it sounds, I think of Charles Dickens and know he would approve. It's been an important part of my being what he described as 'recalled to life'. Then suddenly, amidst all the excitement as we get called up to the starting line, I realise for the first time I haven't seen Maurice and I panic a little, begin to ask the others if anyone's spotted him, but it draws a blank. I try to look for him but we're off and I have no chance to do anything other than start moving forward.

And I do it, running with Maureen, and yes, on our final lap we walk for about a minute but there's so many people encouraging us that we get going again. Pauline runs with us, talking to us all the time. As we cross the finishing line we're cheered home, hugged and congratulated, then as I get my breath back, my phone pings. I'm sure it's going to be Maurice, but it's an email from my daughter and there's a grainy photograph of an early scan showing that everything's all right and she's asking if I'll come and visit them after Christmas, spend time with her during her pregnancy. And, Maurice, forgive me but in the joy of that moment I forget about you and think only of my own child. And even with these weary legs, I'm already starting to run to her.

Maurice

As I put on my royal-blue Fusion Pro quick-dry long-sleeve half-zip running top (extra-large), I think this might be the last time I get to wear it, and I'm a little sad because I've grown quite fond of it. I'm proud that I've come this far, that I've actually completed the nine weeks, and though I'm apprehensive about doing the final run this morning, I know one way or the other I'm going to finish the course, even if I have to crawl on my hands and knees. And I've lost weight so I'm pleased when I need to pull the drawstring on my jogging bottoms really tight to keep them up. I'm eating better and avoiding all fast food. It's helped that in my head I've stopped calling it fast food and now think of it as slow food, part of something that atrophied both my body and my brain into a slow-motion dullness. On the one occasion when I yielded to temptation and stopped for a takeaway,

I felt that Pauline was standing watching me eat and experienced such a sense of guilt that I haven't repeated it.

I know Mina would be proud of me and it brings a renewed sense of sadness that she won't be there to see me do the run. Or that Rachel and Ellie won't be there either. But this morning I try not to dwell on those losses and, after a suitably healthy breakfast that Mo Farah would approve of, I do a few stretches while holding on to a chair in the kitchen. I suspect as I raise my leg then slowly do a squat I probably look more like an inflated Darcey Bussell doing her ballet warm-ups. I drink plenty of water before worrying that I've drunk too much and I'll get caught short halfway round the course, so I go to the loo and try to get rid of it again.

I tie my trainer laces for the third time and wonder if I'll run with Cathy or if she'll suddenly find a turbo-charged burst of hidden energy and stride out after Brendan and Ciara. I don't care what time I do but I don't want to humiliate myself. Then there are so many memories crowding in and demanding access that I'm in danger of being overwhelmed at the very time I need to be steady and balanced.

My phone rings and with a start I see it's Rachel calling. I know, I just know before she even speaks, and my heart is already racing as if I've just done the world's longest run when I hear her say, 'Dad, can you come and get us. Can you come now.' And I don't know how to describe how she sounds when she says those words, but I hear everything I never wanted to hear in my child's voice and, as I start to ask her what's wrong, she cuts across me and repeats, 'Come now please,' so I tell her I'm coming and when the phone goes dead, I tell her again that I'm coming and keep repeating the words as I look for my car keys. Except I can't find them. Can't find them anywhere, and I'm in a panic, my mind blanking out when I need it to be sharp and focused. Afterwards, of course, I remember that having watched a television programme about how car thieves can now scan your keys from outside the house and drive off, I'd started to store them in a metal biscuit tin. But not a single realisation of that fact seeps into my consciousness as I turn the house upside down, more and more desperate, until I say to hell with it and almost flinging the front door off its hinges, burst into the street and start to run.

And I'm not doing any soft-shoe shuffle, not moving sideways like a crab – I'm running – and because there's people walking their dogs on the pavement, and lots of houses haven't bothered to put their bins back in after the Friday empty, I take to the road. I don't care about the people looking at me or the dogs startled into barking. Don't care about a car pumping its horn or a couple of yobs shouting names. Don't care because the only thing ringing in my ears is Rachel's voice, and I know it was a voice shaped by fear and that fear flows into me and it's stronger than the searing pain in my lungs or the complaints from the rest of my body. Her house is five streets away and I'm not half-way there. I try to tell myself that I'm not slowing, silently curse every sick note I ever forged, every games lesson I mitched and every hour I've spent on the couch. And the anger gives me new impetus, enabling me to gulp in more air, to hold it in my lungs before letting it out again, and I try to keep myself upright like Pauline always tells me.

The remaining streets seem to stream past me in a blur, as if it's time itself that has speeded up. And then I'm at the house, where I suddenly realise that I need all my strength, that I don't want to collapse over the finishing line like Roger Bannister doing his four-minute mile, so I pause for a second before I rattle the front door. There is the sound of a lock being turned and a chain moved but the door only opens wide enough to allow her to see that it's me. Wide enough for me to see that one of the eyes looking at me is shadowed and that she has a cut lip.

'Open the door, Rachel,' I say quietly, controlling my breathing and my anger as best I can. But she has it opened before I have finished speaking and so I find myself standing in the hall looking at my daughter who has a black eye and a split lip. Ellie is half-hidden behind her and at the foot of the stairs stand two suitcases and clothes stuffed into plastic bags.

'Where is he now?' I ask, but Rachel shakes her head to say she doesn't know. And it's as if she can't bring herself to look at me.

Then Ellie asks why I'm dressed funny and I kneel down in front of her and tell her that I've been out for a bit of a run. And when I ask her if she'd like to come and stay with me for a while, she smiles and nods, then asks if Mummy can come too.

'Yes, Mummy can come too,' I say and, going to Rachel, I take her in my arms and hold her tightly as suddenly her body goes into a kind of spasm and I think if I wasn't holding her she would collapse.

She doesn't speak but she's crying now and I feel her tears against the side of my neck.

'You're safe now,' I tell her. 'No one's going to hurt you.'

I touch her hair – something I haven't done in a very long time – and then she straightens herself and brushes her tears away with the back of her hand, and down the vista of years I remember the same movement from childhood after she had fallen off a swing and skinned her knees.

'We need to hurry,' she says. 'I don't know when he'll be back.'

And as I look at her wounded face, part of me, a part that I never really knew was there, wants him to come back. Almost wishes he'd walk right through that front door, because there is a molten anger churning inside me, ready to flow out, but then I look at my daughter and grandchild and know this isn't about what might make me feel better, but about helping them to safety. So I lift the two cases and wait while Rachel gathers up the plastic bags. When Ellie insists on being given something to carry, we find her the lightest one, then walk as quickly as possible back to my house.

I know better than to push Rachel into talking about what happened so I just wait until she's ready, and then it comes out gradually and enough for me to understand the world she's been living in, but when I tell her we need to go to the police, she shakes her head. And it takes a long time to persuade her to let me take photographs of her face. When I do she won't look directly at the camera, as if somehow the shame is hers.

A couple of hours later Mark is banging on the front door. And the realisation that he's outside sends Ellie running into her mother's shaking arms and I tell them to go upstairs. I'm not a man who even knows what bravado really means, someone who's managed to get through his life without ever hitting anyone, but I look round hoping to find something to have in my hand when I open it. There's nothing, but I don't go to it empty-handed because I'm holding a new surge of anger.

When I do open it he's ready to brush past me, but I'm good at filling a space so he doesn't make it over the doorstep. And I don't know how to fight, or even how to talk tough, so it must be someone else grabbing him by the throat and rattling his head against the metal door knocker, and someone else telling him that if he steps foot in my house, he'll need someone to carry him expletive deleted out. And I tighten my grip again until his

97

eyes widen, and then I shake him loose and shut the door as he turns on his heels, throwing nothing more than fat-boy curses. When I look round Rachel's standing on the stairs with her phone in her hand and she tells me she's phoned the police. And I'm proud of her. Two hours later he gets arrested and charged with assault and possession of class A drugs with intent to supply.

I give Rachel her own space and she sits with Ellie on the settee while they watch cartoons. I remember the run I was supposed to do and how everyone will secretly believe I bottled it. When the phone rings it's Cathy and I just tell her that I had family stuff to take care of but I think she understands. She's done her run in a slow time but doesn't care and Brendan did it in twenty-two minutes and then went back out to run with Angela. And everyone finished and Yana has asked her about how to apply for university and her own daughter has invited her out to Australia and is paying for the ticket. The news tumbles out and I listen in almost silence, unable to share the excitement.

That evening, after I make my family a meal, we settle down to watch television. About eight, when Rachel is thinking of putting Ellie to bed, we both start as there's a knock on the front door but I reassure us both that it's not him. When I cautiously open it, at first I'm not quite sure what I'm seeing. It's a group of people standing at my front gate and each of them is wearing an LED light on their head, so I think that they're carol singers, but then it's Pauline stepping forward and saying, 'Hi Maurice, it's good you've still got your kit on,' and she hands me an LED. At first I don't understand and when I do Cathy and Maureen say they're all run out and will sit with Rachel if I like, and when I check with her that it's OK, she tells me to go, that she's glad I'm a runner.

As I put on the head torch I see they're all there and I thank them. Then we slip through a side gate into the sleeping park and Pauline asks if I'm ready. They circle round me, hands on my shoulders like I'm a boxer going into the ring, and then we set off, a bright cohort of light moving through the darkness, in a world that is slowly drawing in. And I feel sure that somehow Mina is watching, watching and smiling as I do this dancing in the dark for her, while we run on, banishing the shadows, our lights showing us the way.

A Note on the Type

The text of this book is set in Bembo, which was first used in 1495 by the Venetian printer Aldus Manutius for Cardinal Bembo's *De Aetna*. The original types were cut for Manutius by Francesco Griffo. Bembo was one of the types used by Claude Garamond (1480–1561) as a model for his Romain de l'Université, and so it was a forerunner of what became the standard European type for the following two centuries. Its modern form follows the original types and was designed for Monotype in 1929.